Published by Next Chapter Press
P.O. Box 1937
Boca Grande, FL 33921

Publisher's Cataloging-in-Publication Data
Bryan, Jennifer Liu.

Cole Family Christmas / by Jennifer Liu Bryan with Hazel Cole Kendle. – Boca Grande, FL. : Next Chapter Press, 2008.

p. ; cm. (Cole family)

Summary: Nine children and their parents find true joy one snowy Christmas in the coal mining town of Benham, Kentucky.

ISBN13: 978-0-9816265-0-5

1. Cole family—Juvenile fiction. 2. Christmas—Juvenile fiction. 3. Appalachian Mountains—Juvenile fiction. I. Kendle, Hazel Cole. II. Title.

PZ7 .B79 2008
[Fic]—dc22   2008902106

Printed in Singapore
12 11 10 09 08 • 5 4 3 2

Creative Director: Bob Robbins

Cover and Interior design: Michelle Edmonds, Lynne Desjardins and Bob Edmonds, of Electra Communications
www.ElectraCommunications.ca

Illustrations: Jenniffer Julich
www.jnnffr.com

COLE FAMILY CHRISTMAS

Jennifer Liu Bryan with Hazel Cole Kendle
Illustrations by Jenniffer Julich

Next Chapter Press
Boca Grande, Florida, USA
colefamily-christmas.com

ACKNOWLEDGMENTS

The author would like to thank Candace Kendle, without whom this book would not exist. Thanks also goes to Elizabeth Wilson Walker for her memories and her company on an unforgettable trip to Benham, Kentucky. Phyllis Sizemore, assistant curator at the Kentucky Coal Mining Museum, and Benham resident Paul Graham gave generously of their time and expertise to provide important background for the book. Chris Bergen served as a patient and thorough reader, Rachel Polimeni offered invaluable suggestions, and Lynne Liu gave the sort of great ideas, feedback and encouragement that only a mother could. And finally, enduring gratitude goes to Kendle and Jack Bryan, whose love and support help to make all things possible.

Jennifer Liu Bryan
Alexandria, VA

The illustrator would like to thank Phyllis Sizemore, assistant curator, Kentucky Coal Mining Museum; Theresa Osborne of Southeast Kentucky Community and Technical College; and Benham, Kentucky, residents Linda Fawbush-Halcomb, Charles Sweet, George Smith, and Mary Ann Martin for their guidance in helping her capture the essence of family life in Benham, the look of the town, and coal mining in the early 1900s. Constant gratitude to my husband Tom, my daughter Casey, and my son Austin for their continuing support of my artistic endeavors.

Jenniffer Julich
St. Catharines, Ontario

To learn more about the history of coal mining in Kentucky visit
www.kingdomcome.org/museum

FOREWORD

Christmas has always been a treasured time in my family. When I was growing up, my sister Ruble, the storyteller of our family, often spoke of a very special Christmas that took place when my father was working as a miner and our family was living in the town of Benham, Kentucky. I think back and wonder how, on a coal miner's wages and with so many mouths to feed, Papa and Mama managed to make that holiday both memorable and meaningful. The family never forgot the magic of that special Christmas.

The story that follows is based on my family members' recollections. I hope that you will enjoy reading it as much as the Cole family has enjoyed telling it.

Hazel Cole Kendle

A Shattered Treasure

The Cole house was strangely quiet. Ruble rocked her baby sister in the living room and wondered at its silence. Normally, the small house vibrated with the sounds of its eleven occupants. The doors creaked and dishes clattered, her brothers' and sisters' voices tumbled over one another, and their footsteps pounded against the wood floors.

Ruble shifted sleeping baby Hazel to her other arm. She was just about to get up to investigate the strange stillness when she heard her mother's sweet voice singing softly from the nearby kitchen and the muted sounds of pots and pans clanging together.

Of course. Mama was preparing supper, and Ruble mentally ticked off the rest of the family's whereabouts. Papa was at work. Her oldest sister Maude was sewing in the children's bedroom. Her oldest brother Dock was at his chores outside. Her youngest brothers were napping in her parents' room. Despite the December cold, Al, Nelle, and Hob were at play on the steep slopes of the mountain outside.

Ruble breathed in deeply and sat back to continue rocking Hazel. The stillness was rare, and it wasn't unwelcome.

She took in the quiet living room as if for the first time. The small room seemed empty and cheerless without members of the Cole family sprawled on its furnishings and floor. Every family member had his or her favorite place when they gathered each evening, and then the chill room became warm and cozy, almost hot with all the bodies crammed inside its four

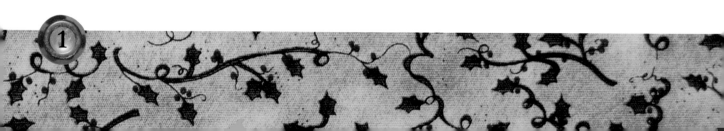

walls. Ruble was sitting in her mother's spot, a wooden rocking chair that creaked and scraped against the room's bare plank floors.

Ruble, ten years old, relished sitting in the chair when she could because it let her gaze at the simple wooden bookcase in the corner of the room that contained the family's few treasures. On the top shelf sat her mother's carnival glass: deep purple bowls with wavy, fluted edges, not unlike waves of water, Ruble thought. At this hour, the three bowls caught the sunlight and threw specks of lavender light into the spare room.

Mama said the glass brought "a little bit of elegance to the old Cole house." Sometimes she said that about Ruble and her sister Nelle, too. The carnival glass was brought out only for special occasions, where it was admired by neighbors in the small coal company town.

Ruble was gazing at the glass, imagining how it had been made, when she heard Al's shout, Nelle's delighted shriek, and her brother Hob's infectious laughter. Their footfalls pounded up the house's wooden stairs and they burst into the room with a waft of cold air and snow, breaking Ruble's reverie. The family's dog, Frank, drawn by the commotion, bounded in, too.

Hob was holding Nelle's scarf high like a victory banner and the three of them were a blur of arms and legs as they each struggled for it, laughing playfully. Their high spirits were contagious, and Frank began to bark with excitement and run in and out of their tangle of limbs. Ruble sucked in a sharp breath as she saw what was about to happen.

The excited dog became caught in the bramble of their wrestling legs and all of them – Al, Nelle, Hob, and Frank – pitched forward precariously. They stumbled as one, lurching right into the wooden bookcase holding the carnival glass. As they fell in a jumble at the foot of the bookcase, Ruble saw a bowl rock back and forth from its perch high on the shelf.

Don't fall, she pleaded silently.

Then the bowl pitched forward. As if in slow motion, Ruble saw it fall to the floor and shatter with a crash.

The children's mirth vanished and the house became silent. They all stared in horror at the remains of the glass bowl, now a mess of candy-like purple shards. Even baby Hazel had awakened and seemed to be looking solemnly at all of them.

In the dreadful silence, Ruble noticed that Mama's singing had stopped. She had quietly come into the room and was standing before them, drying her hands on her apron.

Nelle, looking from her mother to the shattered glass, burst into tears. Frank, sensing the tension, nudged the door open and ran back outside as the boys

scrambled to their feet. They waited soundlessly as they watched Mama take in the scene.

Mama's eyes lingered on the purple shards of glass that were the remains of her once-prized bowl. Her hands stopped their motion on her apron and she said quietly to the room, "Please clean this up and get back to your chores. Papa will be home soon." She gently closed the open front door and returned to the kitchen.

The children looked at each other in stunned silence. Mama's calm reaction to her broken bowl seemed somehow more shocking, and more of a rebuke, than if she had yelled at them. They wordlessly set to work cleaning up the broken glass.

Ruble heard Nelle's stifled sobs as she swept the glass into the dustpan. Nelle was twelve. She and her mother were close, and she knew what the bowls meant

to Mama. Mama had received them as a wedding gift many years before. Since then, the bowls had survived many relocations as the Coles moved from coal town to coal town. But while the youngest family members had trudged on foot over treacherous and rugged mountains, the precious bowls had traveled safely on a train. Every time they'd settled, Mama had carefully unpacked the bowls and set them on a high shelf for display. With such care and vigilance, not one had yet broken, until today.

Ruble took the broom from Nelle. With baby Hazel still in her arms, she embraced her sister, who started to cry in earnest. "I shouldn't have run in here like that. I know better," she sobbed.

"It was an accident, Nelle," Ruble whispered. "Mama knows."

Al squeezed Nelle's arm and Hob patted her on the back. Baby Hazel grabbed Nelle's hair in her tiny fist. "Ow," Nelle said, her sobs breaking into a small smile.

"It was all our faults," eight-year-old Hob said seriously. "I shouldn't have taken your scarf."

Nelle shook her head. "I shouldn't have chased you into the house like that. It was foolish."

"Well, I don't blame any of us," Al said. "It was clearly Frank's fault." He winked to show he was teasing, and as they laughed and fell into a comforting embrace, Ruble saw that the afternoon's commotion had awakened her two little brothers, who stumbled out of their parents' room after their nap. She giggled at the bleary, confused looks on the faces of three-year-old Tony and five-year-old Fos.

"Whatcha doing?" Fos asked grumpily.

"What's wrong with Nelle?" Tony added, noticing her tear-streaked face.

Nelle wiped away her tears and bent to hug little Tony. "Nothing's wrong with me that can't be fixed by a hug," she said. Tony obediently gave her a hug, as did Fos, who impatiently let his sister cover him with kisses before promptly wiping them off.

"There," Nelle said, standing and sighing. "I'll make it up to Mama somehow. Now I'd better go help with supper."

At her cue, the other children also set to work with their before-supper chores. Al, fourteen, went to join his older brother Dock outdoors for the work still to be done, including the evening milking of the family's cow and mucking out its small shed. Hob saw to gathering the odd tables and chairs that the family would cobble together to form their oversized supper table. When Maude, eighteen, finished her sewing, she'd carry out the sewing table that would serve as Ruble's seat. Ruble, for her part, would fold laundry and keep watch over the smallest children, who were now at play on the living room floor.

Ruble groaned as she looked at the large pile of washing Mama had pulled from the clothesline. She had been putting off this chore since she'd gotten home from school; she hated the work of sorting, folding, and putting away all those clothes. She watched with envy as Fos and Tony, carefree, argued over who got to play with a wooden top.

A thought occurred to her and she pulled a sock out of the pile of clothes, holding it up for her brothers to see. "Which of you two can pair up all these socks the fastest?" she asked, looking from Tony to Fos.

"Me!" Fos exclaimed, clambering onto the pile.

"No, me!" Tony yelled, throwing himself on top of his brother. Both boys clawed through the pile, pulling out the socks and setting up rival bundles of pairs.

Ruble looked with satisfaction at the dwindling pile of washing. "Next, let's see who can sort the clothes the fastest. I want to see eleven piles: one for each family member!"

Her brothers silently nodded their assent, concentrating on the laundry game, and Ruble sat back, pleased that she had cut down on some of her work, though she'd still have to fold all those clothes. She breathed in deeply the growing aromas of supper. Soon her father would return from the coal mine.

Indulgently rocking baby Hazel a few more moments, Ruble wondered whether Mama would tell Papa about the broken carnival glass bowl. He wasn't likely to be angry at an accident, but she knew he'd be sorry for the loss of one of Mama's prized possessions. Ruble stared a bit forlornly at the remaining glass bowls on the high shelf and the gap where the shattered bowl had been.

Surprises at Supper

By the time Ruble's father trekked up the narrow and treacherous "holler," the steep incline that led from the mine to the small settlement of homes in the coal town of Benham, Kentucky, he was both black with coal dust and pink with cold.

The family knew he had arrived by the noises preceding his entrance. He always took off his coal-covered boots on the porch, where he noisily clanged them together, throwing clods of black snow onto the porch. Then he shook himself vigorously, removing his hat and rifling his hands through his hair, trying to shake free any remaining black dust. If the children were watching, he'd stick out his tongue in an imitation of a puppy dog shaking itself free of water. But despite washing at the coal mine and dusting himself on the porch, evidence of his dirty work in the mine still entered the house with his every footfall, and the careworn creases in his face still held traces of black.

Two of the littlest Coles, Fos and Tony, ran to greet Papa. As always, he lit up at the sight of them. He tweaked each of their noses with his stained black fingers, leaving sloppy smudges on their pink faces. "My two puppies," he said, as he did every night.

Maude, the oldest Cole daughter, stood back and smiled despite herself. As usual, she had prepared a washcloth to remove the black marks from her brothers' faces. Fos and Tony grinned at one another. "Come here, you two," Maude said playfully. "You have a little something on your noses."

By the time Papa sat down to the supper table, the rest of the family had gathered. Ruble eagerly eyed the steaming bowls of food set around Papa's seat. Despite the rumbling tummies around the table, all of the children patiently waited as their father settled in. Picking up plates one by one, he loaded each with the night's offerings: chicken and corn bread, home-canned vegetables from the family's garden, and potatoes. Every child dutifully passed the full plate to the person next to him and all waited, forks at the ready, until each had been served.

As Papa passed the last plate to his right, Mama handed him baby Hazel and all the children bowed their heads. Their mother's voice rang out like a bell. "For what we are about to receive, may the Lord make us truly grateful." The children called "Amen" in unison, and the next noises were forks clanging against dishware and the satisfied sounds of happy eaters.

"So," Papa said as he balanced Hazel on his lap, feeding her small spoonfuls of supper, "what happened today?"

Nelle, Ruble, Al, and Hob looked from one another to Mama. Would she tell Papa about the broken bowl? Was she angry? Heartbroken? Ruble's heart began to beat a little faster. Mama looked up from her plate and smiled. "Just the usual bedlam of the Cole household."

At this short but cheerful reply, Ruble smiled encouragement at Nelle, who wore a worried frown on her face. Ruble knew that Nelle was still filled with regret. As much as the carnival glass meant to their mother, it might have meant just as much to Nelle. Like Ruble, she had spent many afternoons gazing at it.

Fos piped up, "I lost a tooth."

Papa grinned. "Lost it, eh? Where did you lose it? Did you accidentally swallow it? Better let me take a look down your throat."

Fos shook his head vigorously. "It fell out," he said, pulling down his lower lip to reveal a gap in his teeth.

"I don't know, Fos," Papa said. "Better let me have a look down the hatch."

Fos obediently went to his father's chair, where Papa pretended to examine his little red mouth for the missing tooth. "Hmmm. I don't see it in there," he said, feigning worry. "Perhaps it's already in your belly." His large hand moved to Fos's stomach, where he poked and prodded in an attempt to feel the missing tooth. Fos giggled happily at the attention.

"Phew," Papa said, finally. "I guess you didn't swallow it."

"Mama has it!" Fos burst out. And with that, Mama pulled from her apron a tiny little tooth. The children around the table duly admired it, and Fos puffed out his chest with pride.

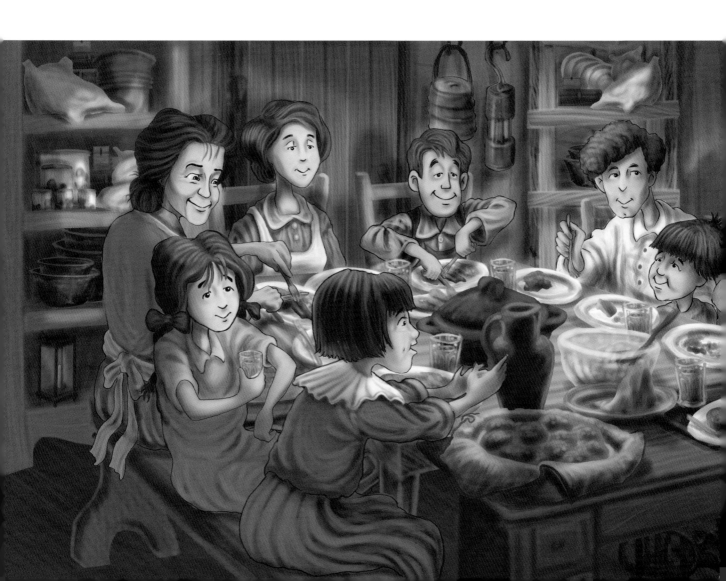

"My, my," Papa said. "That is an exciting thing that happened today."

Dock smiled at his father. "How was your day, Papa?"

"Not so bad, son," he said, turning more sober. "But one of the Lawson brothers was hurt. A coal cart came off the rails and smashed into him. I think he might have broken a rib."

"I'll go check on Mr. and Mrs. Lawson tomorrow," Mama said, her mouth pursed in a look of worry.

Ruble looked at Papa with the same concern. She knew that his job in the coal mine was extremely dangerous. She had seen some of the men in town with bandages on their heads and arms in slings from accidents. Worse, she knew there

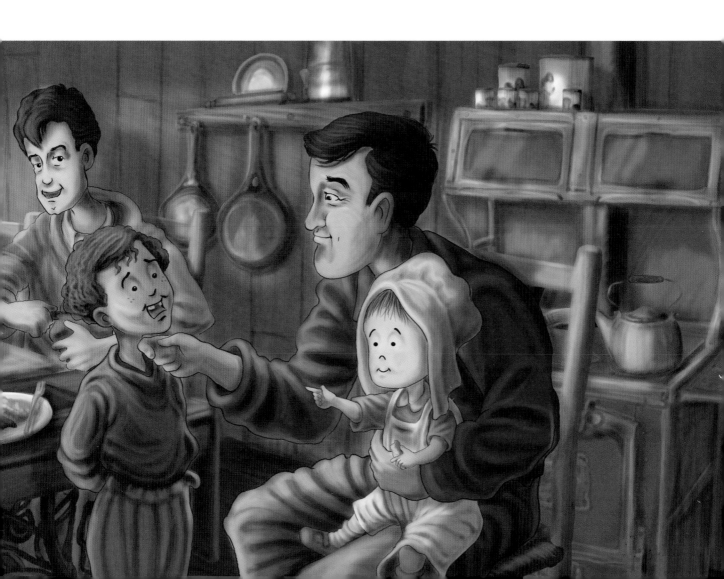

were scarier dangers than loose coal carts. The possibility of an explosion or collapse that could bring down the mine – and the men – was ever present.

Ruble knew, too, that an injury to a coal miner could spell disaster for his family. She fingered the woven bracelet that Brenda Sullivan had given her last month when they had said their tearful goodbyes. A mining accident had crushed Brenda's father's hand. He could no longer swing a pick axe or even set charges in the black coal seam of the mountain. There was no more work for him in Benham, and within a month, the Sullivans had to leave their house to make way for a new worker's family. Ruble didn't know where they had gone, but she remembered the look of despair and worry on the face of Mrs. Sullivan and the forlorn way that Mr. Sullivan had held his crumpled hand inside his coat. Tonight, she saw traces of the same pain on Mama's face.

Ruble looked at her oldest brother, who was talking quietly with Papa about the accident. At sixteen, Dock was already nearly as tall as his father, and Ruble had noticed that his boots, set out by his bed each evening, were even bigger than Papa's. These days, Dock no longer walked in his lumbering gait with Ruble and their siblings down the steep holler toward school. Instead, he hustled around the railroad tracks, collecting iron scraps to sell to the coal company and retrieving the large lumps of coal that fell from the railroad cars.

Ruble remembered the mix of pride and regret on her parents' faces when Dock brought home the coins he'd earned the first day he'd left school to go to work. With eleven mouths to feed, Dock's earnings were essential to the family's survival. Unlike many of the boys in town, however, Dock had stayed in school long enough to learn to read and write. Papa, who could neither read nor write, was proud that Dock had been able to attend school so long. He was prouder still that Maude, the oldest, had so excelled at school that she would go to college next year, a first for the Cole family. Furthermore, she would go tuition-free.

Ruble knew that Dock worried about his father in the mines and that Dock felt a sense of responsibility for the family that weighed on him. "I wonder whether I should work there," he had told Ruble once, "if only to help keep Papa safe."

When Papa returned after bedtime from a late shift at the mine, Ruble could sometimes hear Mama talking to Dock in his bed. "Papa is home. He's safe," she'd whisper, and finally Ruble would hear Dock's steady breathing. He could sleep well only when he knew his father was home.

Papa cleared his throat. He smiled broadly at the table, and Ruble thought he was trying to lighten the mood after the bad news. "I did hear a thing today," he said, "almost as exciting as Fos losing a tooth." He waited as the children's eyes fixed on him in anticipation.

"The company announced that the Christmas party is in three weeks – and of course we're all invited."

At this, all of the children burst into excited conversation. Papa's eyes twinkled at the cheer that now spread around the table. The Christmas party was the highlight of the holiday season and a major event in Benham. All the Cole family's neighbors would gather in their finery and head toward town for the festivities: performances by schoolchildren, choral singing, a play or a skit, a big banquet, and, of course, a stocking full of gifts for every child in town. It was a special time for the town to gather and one of the occasions when the company and its managers were especially generous to their workers and families.

Indeed, the company had already blessed the Cole family this year. Papa had been made a foreman, and his larger paycheck had already been felt in the more generous portions of meat on the supper table and a few small luxuries the family members now allowed themselves. Indeed, Ruble was already thinking about the yellow ribbons Mama had recently given to her. Perhaps she'd weave them into her hair for the party; they matched her best dress.

The din of conversation was interrupted when Mama announced that she, too, had a surprise that she'd reveal after supper.

The children looked at one another. "What is it?" Tony asked.

Mama smiled and shook her head. "I said 'after supper' young man," she teased, tapping her fork on his nearly untouched plate. With that signal, Tony picked up his fork and began to dutifully shove in the food before him – too fast, no doubt, to taste it. Papa laughed.

Dock, on the other hand, his spirits roused by talk of the Christmas party and an after-supper surprise, had put away his worries and cleaned his plate. As was traditional in the hill country, he handed his plate to Papa and said, "I would thank you for some more potatoes."

Al, mouth still full of supper, also extended his plate. "I would thank you for some more, too."

Papa grinned as he heaped more potatoes onto his sons' plates. "Well, Mrs. Cole, with our boys eating like this, I think you'd better plant a bigger garden next year!"

CHAPTER THREE
The Wish Book

aude was in the kitchen heating a bucket of water she had drawn from the nearby stream to wash the dishes in when Ruble crept into the room. The rest of the family was gathering in the living room in anticipation of Mama's surprise.

"Did you save some supper for Hilda?" she asked her oldest sister in a hushed voice.

"Of course. I wouldn't forget her," Maude said, smiling. "You tell that Hilda she's one lucky beast. It's corn bread tonight."

Ruble grinned and took the small sack of plate scrapings Maude held out. She'd have to hurry outside and back if she didn't want to miss Mama's surprise, but she didn't want to leave Hilda without her evening treat.

The night air was cold and biting as Ruble hurriedly trekked the short distance to the small shed where the family's cow – and Ruble's pet goat, Hilda – were sheltered. Ruble tried to keep these visits short because Mama frowned on her evening trips through the cold to, as she said, "spoil a goat, for goodness' sake."

Hilda looked up at Ruble's entrance and immediately bleated and headed toward the bag in Ruble's outstretched hand. "Corn bread, Hilda," Ruble cooed as she scratched the small goat's head. "And none for that mean old cow."

As if it understood her, the family's cow mooed loudly in the small space and started toward Ruble.

"Back off, you," she scolded. "This is for Hilda." The cow ignored her, pushing toward them in the cramped space of the shed. Ruble frowned and turned back toward her beloved pet goat. "I'm sorry you've got to share this barn with this mean dumb cow," she said, looking pointedly at the dairy cow.

As if in response, the cow mooed loudly.

Ruble returned to the house to find the rest of the Coles gathered in the living room. But rather than draped over their usual seats, all had gathered around Mama's rocking chair. Ruble peered over Fos's small shoulders at the package Mama was holding. It was small but substantial, square shaped, and wrapped in plain brown paper.

"Ruble's back!" Fos announced loudly. "Open it!"

Mama glanced at Ruble and shook her head. "Hilda," she said, clucking softly.

Ruble smiled and shrugged. She couldn't help loving her goat.

"What is it?" Fos reminded his mother, pointing at the package impatiently.

"Fos Cole, if you're in such a hurry, why don't you open it?" Mama said, handing him the bundle.

Fos looked at the package in her outstretched hands, now slightly unsure of himself. The responsibility of opening it seemed to dull his excitement a bit.

Three-year-old Tony poked his older brother in the ribs. "Open it, Fos!"

That was all the encouragement Fos needed. His small hands ripped at the paper around the package and within seconds its contents were revealed. "A book?" Fos looked up doubtfully.

"Not just any book, Fos Cole," said Mama, playfully taking it back from him. "It's a wish book."

Nelle clapped her hands in excitement and the older Cole children hooted in recognition. Ruble glanced up at the family's bookcase where a handful of similar books lined one shelf – wish books from years past, some with bindings creased and worn from many turnings of their pages.

"What's a wish book?" Tony asked, straining to see around his siblings' gathered bodies.

"A wish book," Mama began, drawing Tony into her lap, "is a catalogue of thousands of things you might wish for. All of them are listed here, in this wish book, and many of them have pictures, too." She flipped through the book's hundreds of pages so Tony could see. Images of tractors, home furnishings, and clothing flashed past.

"This Christmas, you and your brothers and sisters can look through the wish book to find your most wished-for present," Mama said. "Then we're going to write to Santa to tell him what you've decided. If you're good, he just may grant your wish. Your brothers and sisters can help you, Tony."

At that, the three-year-old stopped his mother's hand as it flipped through the book. "A buggy! And a carriage! Can I ask for a carriage, Mama?"

Mama seemed to consider. "Well, how much does it say those things cost, Tony?"

He peered down at the book, puzzled. Ruble scanned the page and pointed to the bold-faced price for him: "Fifty-nine dollars and eighty-five cents," she read aloud.

Tony's jaw dropped. Even at three, he knew that was a fortune. Indeed, he felt kingly if he were given a penny in script to buy candy at the company store. "That's a lot of money," he said soberly.

"It is," Mama answered. "I think the Cole children should be more modest in what they ask Santa for, don't you? After all, if every good child in the world asked for a carriage, how would Santa afford it? And how would he fit it all onto his sleigh?"

Tony nodded in agreement.

"Think carefully about how good you've been this year when you make your wish," Mama said. "There are plenty of magical things in this book that Santa could bring to some lucky Cole children – if they just look." And with that, Mama searched the book's pages and opened the volume wide, pointing.

"Toys!" Tony exclaimed, banging the page excitedly. "Look Fos, wagons! And whistles! And games! And kites! And engines!" He clambered down from

Mama's lap, lugging the book with him, and he and Fos hunkered down on the floor, excitedly turning pages.

Ruble peered over their shoulders at the wish book. She could already see the dolls featured among the toys. Dressed dolls with fine hair in perfect ringlets, rag dolls with long skirts, and baby dolls with large bright eyes. Her hands itched for their turn to thumb through the book's pages, and she marveled at Mama's extraordinary instructions. The children had never been allowed to select items from the wish book before. Indeed, she thought, things must be improving for the family.

"Move over, Fos and Tony," Hob complained. "Let us have a look, too." He shoved his body in between his younger brothers'.

Fos gave him a shove back and Hob knocked into Tony.

"Hey!" the little boy shouted, pushing back in turn.

Mama clucked from her rocker. "Boys!" she said in a warning tone. "What would Santa say about such behavior?"

The three looked at each other and made room for the rest of their siblings to gather round. Ruble found a place between Al's shoulder and Dock's elbow, and like the rest of the children, gazed in wonder at the wish book.

It had been a long time since Ruble had looked through the family's old wish books, and this new book seemed to contain even more wonders. Every page was gray with tiny type boasting about the product and its seller. Thick black lettering hollered at the reader, announcing "leather stitching," a "great bargain," or products of the "finest quality."

Sketches of shoes, baseball mitts, and clocks littered the pages, and Ruble marveled at the time and effort it would take to compile such a book. Its scale amazed her. For someone accustomed to merely browsing the shelves at the company store, its contents were staggering. To imagine possessing such things! To think of the people who did! It really was magical.

Ruble's gaze fell on a black and white sketch of an impressive phonograph. "Twenty-four dollars for a 'talking machine'!" Ruble exclaimed, pointing. "Can you imagine?"

"If I had twenty-four dollars," Dock chimed in, "I'd buy a bicycle. And I'd get Mama a new sewing machine. And I bet I'd still have money left over."

"Well, I'd buy Mama and Papa a carpet for the living room," said Nelle. "And frilly white curtains like the Petersons have! Wouldn't that look so pretty?"

Hob snorted at the idea of spending such a fortune on home decorations. "I'd buy heaps of toys," he said confidently. "With twenty-four dollars, I could get an iron train engine and a BB gun and loads of other stuff, I bet."

The children were quickly occupied with this new game of how to spend twenty-four dollars. Even Fos and Tony, who had little experience with buying anything, were aghast at how many items they could purchase with this princely sum.

Mama and Papa observed this game with smiles, and Papa squeezed Mama's arm lovingly. "Say, Mrs. Cole," he asked softly, gesturing to the bookcase in the room. "I noticed that one of your purple glass bowls is missing. Where is it?"

Mama sighed softly. "Oh, the children were roughhousing today and it was knocked off the shelf by accident."

Papa raised his eyebrows. "Do I need to give some children a talking to?"

Mama shook her head. "It was an accident. Not to worry, Mr. Cole. It was only a dish."

Ruble, seeing this quiet exchange, glanced at Nelle and saw that she was watching, too. Papa caught their eyes and gave a wink, causing Ruble to smile. Nelle, however, looked downcast. Ruble knew she was thinking sadly of the bowl.

"Say, Hob," Papa said suddenly, interrupting his young son as he continued to page through the wish book. "I think I hear a train a' comin'. Do you hear it, too?"

Hob rose to his feet at the question and his two younger brothers, Fos and Tony, followed suit.

"Yessir! I hear its whistle!" he replied, grinning.

"I hear it, Papa!" Tony nearly shouted.

"Me, too!" said Fos.

With that, the boys ran to the small chest in the room that contained their toys. Fos pulled out a wooden train and Papa joined Tony and Hob in rummaging in the chest, emerging with a toy horse and hand-carved cowboy and sheriff figurines. "I want to be an outlaw," said Hob.

"Me, too!" said Tony.

"I'll be the conductor!" said Fos.

"I guess that makes me the lawman," Papa said.

The four of them crouched on the floor, the younger boys' legs sprawled akimbo as they set up the players for their train heist. Ruble noticed that her father's long body was awkwardly curled up next to them so as not to take up too much room in the small space. But his cramped pose was the only thing that gave away the fact that Papa was no longer a young boy – his face was as happy and animated as those of his three young sons.

Normally Ruble might have joined them in their play, but she seized the opportunity to take a more comfortable seat with the wish book now that the youngest had relinquished it. She eagerly turned the book's pages back to the section of dolls. Her eyes scanned the drawings and she read the elaborate descriptions of each doll's features. She sighed with happiness at the idea of owning such a doll. Could there really be one waiting for her under the tree this year?

Brenda Sullivan had been given one store-bought doll that Ruble had envied tremendously. Unlike Ruble's handmade dolls, with their bumpy rag-doll bodies and button eyes, Brenda's doll had boasted a snowy white porcelain face with painted eyes and ruby red lips. She'd had a pretty yellow ruffled dress and silky hair that Ruble had loved to comb. Of course, Brenda had taken the doll with her when her family moved.

Now, looking at the wish book, Ruble imagined the possibility of owning a store-bought doll of her very own. Despite all the other wonders in the wish book, Ruble knew that she would ask for a doll in her letter to Santa. The only question was, how would she choose? There were so many beautiful dolls. Ruble's fingers caressed the book's pages.

Then Ruble saw her. In the far corner of one of the pages, a tiny illustration showed a simple doll in a pretty ruffled dress. Ruble was drawn to her small puckered mouth. Was that a tiny smile, or a pout? She admired the doll's tight ringlets of curls. "Handsomely dressed doll," the description said. "Flowing blonde curls, jointed body, and moving eyes. A very tastefully gotten-up costume, and the highest grade doll that we sell." Ruble's own hair was dark and straight. Her finger traced the doll's curls.

Ruble's eyes settled on the price: one dollar and fifty cents. Such a sum was an extravagance for a plaything, and the corners of Ruble's mouth turned down slightly. Still, she thought, Mama had said to write Santa for a most "wished-for" gift. The wish book was about dreams, wasn't it? Ruble set her mouth determinedly. "I like this one," she said to Maude, pointing to the small illustration.

"Are you sure you want to wish for a doll?" Maude asked. "You've hardly looked through the book. It also has shoes and other things."

Ruble knew that Maude was thinking of Ruble's school shoes. Not only were they nearly worn out, her big toes were already pressing against their leather tops.

Ruble nodded her head anyway. "I'm sure I want a doll. And I'm sure I'll wish for this one." She read the description to herself again.

"Well then, I'll help you write your letter to Santa," Maude volunteered.

Just then, Al's voice called out over the noise in the living room and his brothers' game. "Mama? Are we going to read tonight?" He was holding a dog-eared novel in his hand.

"Yes, we are, Al," Mama answered. At her reply, the noise in the living room ceased and the boys and their father began to put away their toys. Maude whispered to Ruble, "I'll help you with your letter tomorrow."

The family retreated to the children's bedroom and arranged themselves on the crowded bunk beds, huddling together and drawing Mama's handmade quilts around themselves to keep out the seeping cold. Then the room hushed in anticipation of Mama's reading. Even the youngest of the Coles – Fos, Tony, and baby Hazel – knew to remain silent and still when the family's story hour began.

"She sat at the base of the big tree," Mama began, "her little sunbonnet pushed back…"

Ruble smiled at the feel of her family surrounding her. She felt the warm pressure of Nelle's back against hers as they sat back-to-back for support on the bed they shared. She heard her mother's sweet voice rise and fall in the rhythms of the story, and she heard Hazel's steady breathing as the baby dozed in her father's arms.

Ruble felt a slight draft from the floorboards, which let the cold, snow-laden air into the leaky house, and she pulled the quilt more tightly over her and Nelle. As she sat back, the warm blanket about her shoulders, her thoughts drifted away from the pioneer adventure story her mother was reading.

She thought about the doll in the wish book and her tight yellow curls and her pretty ruffled dress. She thought about her mother's broken bowl and Nelle's sad face. She thought about the upcoming company party and the ribbons she might wear in her hair. She thought about the next day and her pet goat Hilda and her chores. And slowly, slowly, Ruble drifted off to sleep.

Letter to Santa

The next days were filled with excitement as the Christmas spirit took up residence in the Cole household. When the younger children weren't looking through the wish book, they were thinking about their letters to Santa. When they weren't discussing their Christmas wishes, they were talking excitedly about the company Christmas party. When they weren't doing their daily chores, they were making holiday decorations in a sign of the merriment to come.

Ruble felt the pocket of her apron where she had tucked away her letter to Santa. Maude had helped her to write it, and Ruble had carefully re-copied their work onto a clean sheet of paper, free of ink blotches and misspelled, crossed-out words. She took it out to look at it and frowned slightly at her penmanship, a poor imitation of Maude's beautiful sloping letters. But "Dear Santa" she had written clearly, the pressure from the ink pen leaving impressions on the paper.

Mama said that she would mail all the children's letters to the North Pole at once, and Ruble looked forward to the family's trip to the post office in town. Now, the only delay was caused by five-year-old Fos, who was again poring over the wish book while sitting in his mother's rocking chair.

"Ruble?" he asked. "Do you think I should wish for a baseball glove or this toy whistle?"

"I don't know, Fos. They both sound good," Ruble said, smiling at his furrowed brow. "But I thought you said yesterday that you wanted a kite."

Fos frowned. "Yeah. I like that kite, too." He sighed dramatically.

Hob strode into the room and his eyes bulged as he saw his little brother with the wish book open on his lap. "Fos! You still haven't made up your mind?"

Fos looked defensive. "Maude wrote my letter," he said, and pulled it out of the pocket of his overalls. "But I might want to change it."

Hob snorted and plucked the letter out of Fos's hands, ignoring his brother's protests. "It says you want a wooden train engine. What's wrong with that?"

"Nothing, I guess," said Fos, "but there's so much other great stuff in here. I can't decide."

"This is the perfect thing, George Foster Cole," said Hob, using Fos's full given name for emphasis. "Think how great our games will be with that new engine."

Fos beamed at the idea. "Yes. And then I always get to be the 'ducter."

"That's conductor," Ruble said smartly.

Hob and Fos ignored her.

"So, can we mail the letters now, Fos?" Hob asked.

Fos bobbed his head in agreement and shut the wish book loudly.

Hob clapped him on the back. "Let's go collect the others' letters. Maybe we can ask Mama to go to the post office today!" And, in a lower whisper to Ruble as he walked by, "Before he changes his mind again!"

Ruble smiled. "I'll go fetch Nelle's – she's in the kitchen."

Ruble found Nelle covered in a thin layer of flour amid a crowd of pie tins and canned goods. Heat radiated from the large stove that dwarfed the tiny cramped kitchen. Ruble gladly basked in its warmth, but Nelle was sweating as she helped with preparations for the family's supper. Mama was a fine cook and prided

herself on a few specialties, and Nelle's daily chore was to help her prepare the family's necessarily large meals.

Mama had even expanded her repertoire since moving to Benham, learning some Hungarian dishes from their immigrant neighbors. "Who would have thought I could learn to cook Hungarian food in the Kentucky mountains?" she had laughed when her family praised her attempt at a new stew.

Looking around at the chaos that the preparations for supper created, Ruble was glad it was Nelle's chore to help Mama in the heat of the kitchen. After all, it was too cramped for more than a few people to stand in the room at a time.

"Nelle, do you have your letter to Santa? We're going to see if Mama can mail them today," Ruble said, stepping carefully around a large pail of water that Al

had dragged from the stream to the kitchen.

Nelle wiped her floury hands on her apron. "It's in the bedroom in my trunk. Ruble?" she asked, grabbing her sister's elbow. "I can't stop thinking about Mama's glass. Do you think there's a way to make up for the broken bowl? Something we can do for Mama for Christmas?"

Ruble looked at her sister; she knew that the broken carnival glass still weighed on the mind of sensitive, quiet Nelle, despite Mama's reassurances that it was not important. "Of course. We'll think of something. Let's ask Hob and Al, too. And maybe Maude or Dock will have an idea. We have a little time before Christmas."

Nelle sighed her relief, "Thanks, Ruble."

Ruble picked her way carefully through the crowded kitchen to the children's

bedroom. Aside from the living room, this was the largest room in the modest house. But it, too, was small, and made smaller still by the six bodies that slept there and the few trunks that held their possessions. All of the oldest children slept in this room – the youngest slept in their parents' room – and Ruble had to crawl carefully over two cots to reach Nelle's trunk.

Ruble opened her sister's trunk and marveled at the neatly packed clothes. Her own trunk was messy. As she pulled out Nelle's letter to Santa from beneath a bulky sweater, she heard a tinkle of glass. She peered into the trunk and noticed a small lumpy bundle. She looked around to see whether Nelle was near, and then she pulled out the bundle and opened it.

Inside were the shards of purple glass from Mama's shattered bowl. "She kept them?" Ruble wondered aloud, surprised. She turned a large purple shard over in her hands. It caught the light from the window and gleamed prettily.

Jealousy suddenly bloomed in Ruble's heart. Why should Nelle have the only keepsakes of the valuable bowl? And why hadn't she offered to share the broken glass with Ruble, too? After all, Ruble had admired the bowls nearly as much as Nelle.

Ruble looked at the shard of glass in her hand and wanted badly to keep it. She could still hear Nelle working in the kitchen. Nelle won't miss one shard much, she thought defensively. It's just a piece of broken bowl.

Ruble moved to her own trunk and shoved the shard deep under her piles of clothes. Then she quickly retied the bundle of glass and placed it carefully back in Nelle's trunk.

Ruble's heart was still racing, her face flushed with guilt, several minutes later when she dashed outside to deliver the letters to Mama, who was milking the cow in the shed. The frigid air felt good, and Ruble hoped it would remove the redness in her cheeks.

"It's going to be very cold tonight from the feel of things," Mama said as she looked up from the cow. "You should put on more clothes when we walk to the post office. If we hurry, we can meet Papa as he gets off from his shift at the mine. We can all walk back to the house together."

Ruble clapped her hands at the idea of surprising Papa. She moved toward the house to bundle up for the walk, but the thought of the cold made her turn back toward the shed. "If it's really freezing, can Hilda stay in the house?" she asked her mother, gesturing toward her goat.

"You know how I feel about goats in the house," Mama answered.

Ruble clamped her lips together. Mama did not like Hilda in the house, but Ruble could often convince Papa to let the goat shelter in the crowded children's bedroom. "Well," she whispered to herself, "I'll ask Papa then and see what he says. He almost always lets her stay in the house. I think he loves her almost as much as I do." Ruble looked down the mountain with excitement at the thought of soon seeing Papa.

Merry Preparations

The morning of the Christmas party, Ruble was awakened by a rough push that sent her tumbling out of bed. "Hey!" she shouted, startled.

Her goat, Hilda, was standing beside her bed. Now she began to bleat and panic as she became tangled in Ruble's sheets and quilt.

"Ruble, is your goat in here?" Dock called groggily from atop a bunk bed.

"There's a goat in here? As though it isn't already crowded enough!" exclaimed Al over the noise of Hilda's bleating.

Mama and Papa pushed open the bedroom door, trailing Fos, Tony, and Frank, the dog. "What's going on here?" Mama asked.

"There's a mad goat on the loose!" Al answered.

Ruble grabbed the rope around Hilda's neck and tried to calm her. "She just got scared. I shouted when she accidentally pushed me out of bed."

Fos and Tony clambered onto the bed to stroke Hilda, but succeeded only in agitating the goat more. She began to bleat loudly and kicked over Al's trunk. Frank began to bark, adding his excited yelps to the din.

Now Papa began to laugh, alarming Hilda further.

Mama, on the other hand, stood in the doorway holding Hazel and shaking her head. "This is why we don't keep goats in the house," she said, but she wasn't looking at Ruble. Mama knew that Papa, an animal lover through and through, had once again given into Ruble's entreaties that Hilda be allowed inside for the night.

By now, Papa had managed to calm Hilda and he led her to the doorway and outside. "All right, Hilda," he said to the animal, "You're fine. And Mrs. Cole says no more overnight stays in the house." But Papa bent to nuzzle the goat's neck and Frank followed the two of them out, wagging his tail happily.

"That old goat," Mama said, looking at Papa's retreating back. She shook her head once more.

Ruble was a little sad to see her goat go, but she did rub her bottom where Hilda had butted her hard. "I hope she'll be all right out there in the cold," she said to no one in particular.

"She'll be all right," Mama said as she turned to leave. "She's a goat, after all. And goats live outside – except this one, for some reason!"

Ruble frowned, but her concern for Hilda was quickly pushed to the back of her mind by preparations for the company Christmas party later that afternoon. She and her siblings raced through their morning chores and talked constantly of the festivities to come.

Nelle finished helping Mama with the potluck offering the family would bring to the party and came into the bedroom to help Ruble and Maude dress Tony and Fos.

"What will you wear, Maude?" Ruble asked her oldest sister. She admired Maude's tall frame and dark hair swept up into a simple bun.

Maude sighed, the corners of her mouth turning down slightly. "I don't know. I haven't much to wear. And I think I'll have to make some new clothes before I go to college," she said, picking listlessly through her trunk. "All these dresses are so worn."

"What about this one? This used to be your favorite," Nelle chirped, holding out a faded but pretty blue dress.

"Yes, Maude," Ruble encouraged as she buttoned Fos's shirt. "You look awfully pretty in that dress."

Maude smiled at her sisters and wiped her hands on her apron, as if ridding herself of some sad thoughts. "Yes, that dress will do just fine. I do like blue, you know. And what will you two wear?"

Ruble and Nelle looked at each other and giggled with excitement. "I'm going to wear my yellow dress," declared Ruble, "and I want to wear my new yellow

ribbons, too! Can you weave them into my hair, please Maude?"

"Of course," she said. "And Nelle, what about you?"

"Oh, my green dress to go with my fancy shoes!" said Nelle, pointing at her feet.

Ruble looked down to see shiny patent leather Mary Janes gleaming on Nelle's rather large feet.

"I never get to wear them, but I think they're so pretty, don't you?" The excitement of dressing up animated Nelle's features.

"They are," said Maude, "but don't you want to wait to put them on until later? They might pinch your feet."

Nelle beamed and shook her head, doing a little jig with the shoes for effect.

Just then Al, already dressed for the party, poked his head into the bedroom. "What are you girls doing in here?" he mock-whined, pretending to look at a pocket watch.

Three-year-old Tony, who was now having his unruly hair wetted and combed by Maude, said with a sincere expression, "We're picking out our fancy dresses."

"I see," Al said, his mouth going into a crooked grin. He playfully grabbed Hob, who had walked into the bedroom all dressed for the party. "Oh, Hob," he said in a high-pitched imitation of his sisters' voices, "you look just bee-yoo-tiful in that coat!"

Hob, catching on, pretended to blush shyly. "Not as ravishing as you look in those shoes!" he returned in an equally high-pitched voice.

"Thank you so much!" screeched Al, pretending to preen. The boys continued to exchange exaggerated compliments, sending Fos into stitches, while Nelle and Ruble shot all of them dirty looks.

Little Tony, however, looked insulted. He had, after all, endured the discomfort of being stuffed into his dress clothes and made to stand still as Maude painfully combed his knotted hair. "What about me?" he shouted loudly over their game. "I look pretty, too!"

This comment sent Al howling out of the room and elicited peals of laughter from the girls.

"Yes, Tony," Ruble reassured him, blinking back tears of laughter. "You look absolutely lovely."

CHAPTER SIX

The Christmas Party

he snow was falling in a thick curtain as the Cole family trudged into the heart of Benham. Mama and Papa were already in deep conversation with some other parents whom they'd encountered making the trip down the mountainside. Children who weren't weighed down with casserole dishes and pie pans were throwing snowballs. The heavy snowfall was very unusual, and Ruble's siblings delighted in kicking their boots through the gathering drifts.

Ruble slowed her pace as the family neared town to admire the sight. Through the haze of snow she could see the twinkling lights and familiar outlines of Benham's company store, the Protestant church, the infirmary, and the boarding house for bachelor miners. Normally the buildings were more practical than cheerful-looking, but today their roofs were covered in a blanket of fresh white snow and their windows glowed warmly against the darkening sky, giving them a cozy appearance. Doorways were draped with greenery for the holiday.

The centerpiece of the town was the huge illuminated Christmas tree glowing in the middle of Center Park. The electric bulbs, powered by the mountain's abundant coal, twinkled merrily in the dusky light of early evening.

Ruble's mouth twitched into a smile at the extraordinary sight. Before the family had moved to Benham, Ruble had seen the bright glow of an electric light bulb only a handful of times. Now she marveled at an entire evergreen tree festooned in white light.

From several paces ahead, Papa's voice called back to Ruble. "This snow is something, isn't it, Tater?" He slowed his gait to let his daughter catch up with him.

"Yes, Papa," she said, taking his offered hand. "How much more do you think we're going to get?"

"Dunno. But if it keeps up this way, we're going to have a tough climb getting home." He gestured toward the steep road.

Ruble's gaze followed his finger, which was pointed toward the cluster of homes perched halfway up the mountain. Her teeth suddenly began to clatter as a gust of wind crept under her coat.

Papa put his arm around her and pulled her closer. "Not to worry, Tater. I won't let anything happen to you," he said. "At least not till after Christmas." He laughed at his joke and Ruble giggled with him. The pair of them were the last of the Coles to enter the church.

Nelle was adding the family's pumpkin pie to a long table crowded with desserts in a room behind the church's sanctuary. Ruble licked her lips at the sight of cookies, cakes, and assorted other treats crammed onto the red and green tablecloths, and she wasn't the only person hovering over the dishes. She was about to inspect the main courses when Fos and Tony ran over to her, trailing colorful Christmas stockings.

"Look, Ruble!" Fos said, waving his stocking in front of her. "We all got stockings from Santa!"

"What's inside of them?" she asked, looking at the lumpy striped fabric.

"We're not 'posed to open 'em until Christmas, silly," scolded Tony.

Fos, nevertheless, began to squish his stocking enthusiastically. "I think I feel a whistle," he said, his tongue sticking out in concentration. "And maybe a candy cane!" He took a big whiff of the knitted material, making Ruble laugh.

"Smell it!" he ordered Tony, who obeyed with a serious expression.

"It smells like cin'man," said the three-year-old solemnly. "Do you think there's cin'man in there, Ruble?"

"There might be cinnamon in there, Tony," she answered. "I guess you'll have to wait until Christmas morning to find out."

Papa and Mama walked over and Papa raised his eyebrows at his young sons, who were now both vigorously pawing their stockings. "Young men," he said in a mock warning tone. They quickly dropped their stockings to their sides. "Let's find a place to sit so this Christmas feast can begin."

"Then can I have my pie?" asked Tony, who had been eyeballing Mama's pumpkin pie since it had emerged, fragrant, from the oven this morning.

"Yes, Tony Cole. Then you can have pie. After you eat your supper, of course," Mama said.

Ruble thought there was a hint of pride in Mama's voice at her son's preference for her pie above all the other temptations piled on the dessert table. Ruble, for her part, planned to sample as many sweets as she could. She lingered for a moment over the dessert table, breathing in its aromas.

But after Ruble had eaten her way through a plate laden with potatoes, turkey, cranberry sauce, ham, fried chicken, and canned greens, she felt a little sick. It was only with great effort that she could swallow a narrow sliver of Mama's pumpkin pie and some fruitcake.

Dock looked ravenously at the cookies and cake that remained on her plate. "Ruble?" he asked, wiping crumbs from his wide mouth. "Are you going to eat that?" He pointed to her abandoned desserts.

Ruble wordlessly shoved the plate over to her brother.

"Heavens!" Mama exclaimed, eyeing Dock's wiry frame. "Where does he put it all?"

Dock grinned and pointed to his mouth. "Right here, Mama!" And with that, he shoved a huge forkful of Ruble's unfinished dessert down, swallowing loudly for effect.

Yet when the meal finally concluded, even Dock looked a little uncomfortable. "Shall we go over to the store?" Papa asked, looking around at his groaning children. "I think a little walk before the evening's entertainment might do us some good."

The children assented readily and piled their winter clothes back on for the short walk to Benham Store. In the brief time they had been indoors for the potluck, the sky had darkened with more storm clouds and the character of the snow had changed from lazy, fat flakes to smaller, harder pinpricks of ice. Papa gave a worried glance skyward as he held the door of the store open for his family.

The two-story structure was already crowded with coal miners and their families browsing the shelves before the next round of festivities began. The Cole children quickly spread out as they encountered school friends and combed the store's wares for new offerings.

Ruble headed over to the store's small selection of dolls. Although she had seen them all before, she inspected them closely, looking at their porcelain faces and examining their machine-sewn dresses.

Yes, she concluded, the doll she had wished for from the wish book was finer than any of the dolls the company store offered. Ruble imagined that her doll's hair was silkier, and her dress still fancier. Her heart quickened again at the thought that maybe – just maybe – she might receive her hoped-for doll. She was turning shyly to ask Mama about the possibility when Al approached with a book in one hand.

"Look, Mama," he said, "they have a new book by John Fox Jr. and a bunch of others."

Mama took the book from Al and examined it. Among the few possessions in abundance in the Cole household were books, and Ruble knew that if her parents were likely to buy anything in the store, it was a novel. "It's a bit expensive yet," said Mama softly to Al, who was the biggest fan of adventure stories in the family. "Maybe we can order it from the lending library."

Al nodded and went back to browse the books. Ruble noticed, however, that Mama did not put down the book and instead tucked it under her arm.

Maude came over and asked whether Mama would join her in looking at fabrics. "I want to look for some new material before I leave for college," she explained. "I would love something like the dress you have on." Maude looked admiringly at Mama's dress, a dark navy with small but bright red roses throughout.

"Why thank you, Maude. I haven't worn this dress in a long time," Mama said. "I'm sure we'll find something fetching for my beautiful girl." Maude blushed.

When she'd gazed long enough at the dolls, Ruble joined Hob and her younger brothers, who were huddled around a bin full of toys. Hob was scrutinizing some carved figures, not unlike the ones the boys played with at home.

"What do you think, Hob? Did you wish for more cowboys from Santa?" Ruble asked.

"Nah. I like the ones that Papa carves," Hob replied, tossing the figures back into the pile. "I think his are even better than the ones the store has. Someday I'm going to learn to carve like Papa."

Their father had sidled up behind them and overheard Hob's high praise. He picked up the surprised eight-year-old and kissed him roughly on the neck. "So, I have a budding wood worker, do I?" he asked as he released Hob and ruffled his hair.

"I'd like to learn, Papa," Hob said.

"Well, then, I'll teach you," replied Papa. "Let's go look at the carving knives."

But as the two of them turned to inspect the knife case, they noticed that the store was emptying of people. Families were moving toward the doors and out into the darkening evening and the Cole family followed.

As they emerged from the warm store into the cold air, Ruble could already hear what was drawing the crowd. A group of church singers had gathered around the wide base of the glowing Christmas tree at the center of town and the strains of "Silent Night" could be heard.

Ruble was surprised when her mother took her hand. "Come on, Ruble," she said. "This is what we've been practicing for in church."

They quickly made their way to the tree and Ruble squeezed into the growing circle of singers beside her mother. As their voices soared to the notes of "Hark the Herald Angels Sing," Ruble thought she could hear her mother's soprano rising above the rest, its rich tones arcing skyward.

Soon Ruble was aware that the rest of her family had gathered around them and she heard the song swell as the assembled townspeople added their voices to the more practiced sounds of the choir. For what seemed like a long time, the people who lived in Benham, Kentucky, sang Christmas carols around the brilliantly lit tree at the center of town.

When the cold snow and a driving wind conspired to force the singers back into the warmth of the church, Ruble helped Tony and Fos pull off their winter coats and then shook out her own freezing limbs. She and the children watched in anticipation as an impromptu stage was readied for a Christmas nativity skit at the front of the church.

"Where's Papa?" Al asked suddenly, looking around.

Ruble scanned the church along with the rest of her family, searching for him. "There he is," she said, noticing him standing huddled with some other coal miners and one of the company managers. "He's coming back."

Papa walked back to his family's pew with a slight furrow on his brow, which he quickly replaced with what Ruble thought was a forced smile. "Well, Cole family," he said, "it looks like Old Man Winter had a meeting with Father Christ-

mas. They're going to break up the party a little early this year so the families can get safely home before the snow piles up too much more. There won't be a nativity skit this year."

As he spoke, Ruble saw one of the big bosses of the company climb to the lectern in front of the nativity actors who were still readying their costumes. He announced the early end to the party to a chorus of groans and boos. Even a few hearty "Ho ho hos" added to the end of his speech could not dispel the glum mood that settled over the crowd.

"Dock," Papa said, putting his hand on his oldest son's shoulder, "I need you and Mrs. Cole to lead the family back up the holler to the house."

"Are you coming, Mr. Cole?" Mama asked, her tone concerned.

"Well, with all this snow, they want to load up the last train early tomorrow so it can roll out of here," he said. "They've gotten word that this blizzard is shutting down sections of the railroad. If I stay down here with the Lawsons, I won't have to wake the whole household in the middle of the night and I can be sure to make it to work. It will be worth it," he added meaningfully, looking at his wife. She nodded, understanding. The Cole family needed the money, especially at Christmas time.

So Mama put on a smile and said brightly to Dock, "Do you think we can get these Coles back up the coal mountain?"

Following her lead, Dock grinned and replied, "I'll bet we can go up faster than we did coming down."

The Cole family bundled themselves back up against the bracing cold and made their way out into the snowy evening once more. Ruble shuddered as the wind whipped at her cheeks, and she blinked against the snow that gathered on her eyelashes.

Papa kissed each of his children on both cheeks and whispered, "I love you. Merry Christmas." He then approached Mama and talked to her in hushed tones while Ruble watched with wide eyes.

"Our Christmas delivery hasn't arrived yet," he said quietly. "With this snow, I'm not sure when it will come." Papa noticed Ruble watching them and lowered his voice further. "I picked up a few things from the store – just in case." Then he embraced Mama and surreptitiously handed her a small bundle.

"What's that?" Fos asked, pointing to the package Mama was attempting to conceal.

"George Foster Cole, you are a nosy little man," Mama said. "It's none of your business."

Fos knew from the tone of her voice not to pry further, but he poked his little brother and pointed at the bundle. "Presents!" he hissed.

"It's a shame the evening had to end so early," Maude said to her mother, taking baby Hazel from her.

"Oh, I don't know," said Mama, brushing snow from the baby's hat. "It's probably a good idea with this terrible weather. I don't know if I've ever seen a storm quite like this. I'm only sorry we didn't get to see the nativity story," she sighed. "It's my favorite part of Christmas."

Ruble saw Nelle's eyes grow wide at Mama's words. She ran over to Ruble and whispered excitedly in her ear, "I finally know what we should do for Mama for Christmas!"

Waiting for Papa

usts of bitterly cold wind caused the Coles' wooden house to creak and groan that night. The fearsome moaning woke Ruble, and she nestled closer to Nelle for warmth and comfort. When Christmas Eve morning finally dawned, she unwound her arm from around Nelle and crawled out from beneath the quilt to see the storm's damage.

The children's warm breath had caused the small window to frost over, but Ruble wouldn't have been able to see much anyway: the wind had driven snow-drifts all the way to the highest pane of glass.

When the rest of the children awoke, they set to their morning chores. Aston-ishingly, snow continued to fall throughout the morning, though not as furiously as it had overnight. Worse were the winds. They howled down the chimney and bent the snow-covered limbs of nearby trees. Gusts kicked up eddies of snow to sting the eyes of anyone who ventured out.

Ruble shivered as she watched Dock trudge into the stark whiteness through knee-deep snow to milk the cow. When he made his way back to the house, he hung lengths of rope stretching from the cow barn and the outhouse to help the family find their way through the deep drifts and stinging winds. Ruble's skin stood out in goose bumps at the thought of venturing into the cold for a trip to the outhouse, though she knew she'd eventually have to.

Before long, Al and Dock had built a roaring fire and the small house grew warm as it filled with activity. After the children finished their morning chores, Nelle recruited them into her plan to produce a family play of the Christmas

nativity story as a gift for their parents.

Fortunately, Mama had closeted herself in her bedroom after breakfast, explaining that she was "working on a Christmas surprise" and was not to be disturbed. The children didn't have time to speculate much on her surprise, because they were distracted by preparations for the play.

"Baby Hazel will play Jesus," Nelle said to her assembled brothers and sisters. "And Dock will be Joseph. Maude, you'll play Mary."

"I want to be the innkeeper," said Al.

"That's fine," said Nelle, grinning at her brother's enthusiasm. "Then Hob, Tony, and Fos, you can play the three wise men. And Ruble, you can be an angel."

"Who will play the animals?" Ruble asked, thinking of her goat in the cold cow barn. "I could bring in Hilda…"

"So she can knock you on your rear again?" Al interrupted, chuckling.

Ruble stuck out her tongue. "Maybe she'll knock you on your rear, Al Cole."

By early evening, the Cole children had figured out their assigned roles and converted the living room into a makeshift stage. They had set Hazel's cradle in front of the mantel, which would do for a manger, and Maude and Dock had donned sheets for Mary and Joseph's traditional garb.

"Should we take down the stockings? It's strange to have them hanging in the manger," Nelle remarked, eyeing the nine stockings from the company Christmas party that swung in front of the fireplace.

"No!" Fos nearly shouted. He ran over to his stocking as if to guard it. "I like seeing all the stockings," he said defensively.

Maude laughed. "I think it's all right, Nelle. It makes the manger...festive!" she said.

Meanwhile, Mama had finally emerged from the bedroom. She viewed the children's stage and costumes with raised eyebrows. "My, you children have been busy this afternoon," she said. "Please get started on your chores now. I hope Papa will be home soon, and I've got to get to fixing supper."

The children shed their costumes and began their evening chores. Ruble helped Hob slide furniture around the living room to create the family's supper table. As she stood before the window, gathering forks and knives from a drawer, she looked out into the cold once more. Without the play to distract her, she could hear that the wind still howled against the side of the house and she saw Dock

struggling through the icy snowdrifts as he again fought his way to the cow barn. Seeing him struggle to open the door against the cold winds, Ruble thought of Hilda and imagined her shivering in the small dark shed.

Ruble crept into the kitchen. "Mama?" she said cautiously. Her mother had her back to her and was busy preparing supper. "Can I let Hilda into the house? It's so cold outside and I…"

"No, Ruble," Mama said firmly. "Your goat will be fine in the shed." Mama turned and looked at Ruble's worried face and gave her a reassuring hug. "Goats are fine in barns and sheds, even in cold weather. Look at the cow: it winters out there every year, through rain and snow. It's not harmed in the least. And neither will Hilda be."

Ruble sniffed and nodded her head somewhat doubtfully. "All right," she sighed.

Ruble finished setting the table, stealing occasional worried glances out the window and thinking of her goat. Before long, supper was ready and evening was darkening the windows, but Papa still had not returned. The family gathered in the living room, waiting awkwardly for him, the merry atmosphere of earlier in the day replaced by an apprehensive stillness.

Ruble began to feel very guilty that she had been so preoccupied with concern for her goat. Now she imagined her father fighting his way up the wind-blown mountain through knee-deep, icy snow. The few minutes she had trekked outside to use the outhouse had chilled her to the bone. To think of her father in such weather – and now in the dark – made her shiver, and not from the cold.

Mama cleared her throat, breaking the silence. "I imagine that Papa is working late after all. Or he might be having a hard time walking up the mountain through this snow," she said at last, looking distractedly out at the winter landscape. "I'm sure he wouldn't want us to wait."

Fos rubbed his rumbling belly. "Good," he said, "I'm starving."

As they ate, even Fos's and Tony's happy stream of talk about their Christmas wishes couldn't cheer the mood. Indeed, Mama seemed to frown at the mention of the wish book. Eventually, even the youngest Coles fell silent, sensing the tense atmosphere and the long gazes at Papa's empty chair.

"Could something have happened to him?" Nelle finally asked, tentatively and quietly. She seemed to almost choke on the words.

Ruble had been fearful to ask the same question. Indeed, she had been pushing her food around her plate, growing more and more frightened about Papa's absence. It wasn't just the cold, she thought as she sat and worried. It was the job he had gone to do. Ruble knew enough about coal mining to be fearful of almost all its aspects: Papa could have been hurt unloading the coal from the depths of the mountain. There could have been a collapse, or an explosion. He could have been injured manning the carts that carried the coal to the surface. They could come off the rails and crush a man. He could have been killed loading coal into the railcars. Accidents were frequent and the work treacherous. Ruble swallowed the lump that rose in her throat.

"No," Mama said more loudly than she intended. Then more quietly, "Papa is fine. We would know by now if it were…something else."

"Shall I go look for him, Mama?" Dock asked.

"Absolutely not," she said firmly. "No more Coles are going out into the snow. Your Papa is sure to be back by morning, if not sooner. In fact, he probably saw the snow and decided to stay another night with the Lawsons. Yes, I'm sure that's what happened. He'll be back tomorrow and wishing us all a Merry Christmas, I know."

Mama gazed around the table at the half-eaten suppers and solemn faces and

seemed to decide something. "In the meantime," she said, opening her hands and forcing a smile, "I want the rest of the Cole family to enjoy their Christmas Eve supper. This is a time of celebration and joy. Christmas is tomorrow. Don't worry about your papa, children. I know he will come home safely."

With that, she forked a piece of supper into her mouth and swallowed it down, allowing a wide smile to light up her face. The youngest Coles, sensing the change in mood and reassured by Mama's words, began to happily eat and chatter once more. Mama gave Ruble's knee a squeeze under the table and smiled at her. "Eat," she said to her daughter.

Ruble nodded. She did her best to let Fos's and Tony's cheerfulness lift her spirits and push dark thoughts to the back of her mind. Finally, the familiar sounds of supper – talking, laughter, and forks and knives clattering – returned to the Cole household.

After supper, Mama refused to let anyone wait up for Papa and sent all the children – even Maude and Dock – to bed. Fos and Tony were wound up for Christmas the next day and still talking about their letters to Santa, the wish book, and the contents of their stockings when Ruble helped tuck them into bed.

"What do you think is in my stocking, Ruble?" Tony asked for the twentieth time.

Ruble smiled at the question. "I don't know, Tony. But I do know that you're going to find out first thing tomorrow." She gave Tony a hug that lingered just a little long.

Tony grinned up at her. "Merry Christmas, Ruble," he said, returning her squeeze with all his three-year-old might.

Mama's voice rang out. "Fos, quit bouncing around on your bed, young man. Don't you want to be well rested for Christmas morning?"

At this, Fos allowed himself to be tucked under the sheets. "Mama?" he asked as she brushed a shock of black hair away to kiss his forehead. "Do you think I'll get my train tomorrow after all? I've tried very hard to be good."

Mama pursed her lips slightly and sighed just audibly. "I'm afraid that Santa may have a hard time getting through all this snow," she said at last. "But if there's a way, Santa will find it."

Maude chimed in from her cot in the other bedroom, "Anyway, Fos, remember what we talked about? The fun thing about wishing is the dreaming. A wish is a hope, not a promise, remember? Whether you get your train tomorrow or not, you've had fun thinking about it every day."

Mama walked to the door and smiled at her oldest daughter. "That's wisdom, Maude."

"I guess," said Fos, doubtfully. "But I think playing with a train would be more fun than wishing for it."

Mama came around to kiss all her children goodnight. When she bent to whisper "Merry Christmas" to Ruble, her daughter caught her hand. "Papa?" she asked in a low voice.

Mama squeezed her hand in response. "He is all right, Ruble," she answered in the same low voice. "Say a prayer to see him home safely. And sleep tight."

But Ruble couldn't sleep. Dock was moving restlessly in his bed, and even after their siblings' breathing was steady and quiet, she lay awake. At last, when the wind ceased its howling and the night seemed still and eerily silent, Ruble rose and peeked out from the bedroom.

Mama was rocking in her chair in the living room, looking out the window that shone from the moon's reflection on the snow, a worried frown etched on her brow.

Ruble knew she was waiting for Papa.

Normally on Christmas Eve, Ruble might have drifted off to sleep thinking of the presents that awaited her in the morning. She might have thought of her wished-for doll and imagined what it would be like to open her present and see yellow ringlets and a pretty dress. She might have dreamed of brushing the doll's hair, kissing its painted red mouth, and pretending to serve it tea.

But that night, Ruble didn't think of her wished-for doll at all. As she pulled the sheets around her, she thought of Papa and her family and she said a deep, heartfelt prayer. The only thing she wanted for Christmas the next day was to see Papa again.

CHAPTER EIGHT

Christmas at Last

ilda's strong push sent Ruble tumbling out of bed on Christmas morning. "Ow," she cried out, surprised awake. How on earth had this happened? How had Hilda gotten in?

As the other children began to stir, Ruble threw her arms around Hilda and then stopped, thinking. Mama had said Hilda was not allowed in the house. If the goat was in her room, then perhaps…

"Papa!" Ruble shouted. She got up from the floor and ran out into the living room,

trailed by her groggy brothers and sisters who were also stumbling out of bed.

The living room seemed transformed for Christmas. The small green tree that the family had placed near the fireplace was now festooned with colorful ribbons and hung with the children's homemade ornaments. A roaring fire warmed the room and drew notice to the bulging stockings on the mantle. But Ruble's eyes quickly found what she was looking for: Mama and Papa stood beaming before her, hanging the last few ornaments on the tree.

"Papa!" Ruble shouted with joy, running into his open arms. The rest of the Cole children followed suit and soon nothing more of Papa could be seen but the top of his head as his children enveloped him.

Ruble, her arms encircled around her father, felt all of her brothers and sisters close in around her and knew happiness. As they pulled away, Ruble saw Papa quickly brush a few tears from his eyes. Mama's eyes had welled up, too.

"Where have you been?" Tony said accusingly to Papa, to laughter from the rest of the family.

"You're right to scold me, Tony. I missed all of you terribly!" Papa said, squeezing Mama's hand. Ruble could see dark circles under her eyes, evidence of a long night. "Our shift ran very long, and then I had a little trouble getting back up the mountain after that snowfall yesterday. You know, folks in town say this is the worst storm in a hundred years."

Gazing out the window, Ruble had to agree. The snow had drifted up one side of the house, obscuring a window entirely. On the other side of the house, the winds had piled snow into banks. Ruble shivered a little despite the warmth of the room. She felt compelled to hug her papa once more, she felt so grateful that he was safe.

"The tree looks beautiful, Mama and Papa," Maude said, circling an arm around her mother. At this remark, Nelle clapped her hand over her mouth.

"I almost forgot," she said, skipping off to the bedroom. She returned a moment later, delicately carrying a few shards of purple glass with ribbons carefully attached.

"For the tree," Nelle explained to Mama's surprised expression. "I couldn't bear to throw any of your bowl away."

Ruble watched, shamefaced, as her sister tied the few remaining shards of glass onto the tree. Like the bowl once had, they threw sparkles of lavender light into the room.

Mama smiled and kissed Nelle on the forehead. "They are perfect. What a wonderful idea," she said.

Seeing this, Ruble's cheeks reddened. She slipped into the bedroom and rum-

maged through her trunk, emerging with the shard she had taken. "Nelle, here's one more for the tree," she said quietly, handing her sister the large purple piece. "I took it from your trunk the other day. I…I wanted to keep a piece of the bowl, too," she stammered, her eyes watering. "I'm sorry."

Nelle smiled her forgiveness. "It's all right, Ruble." The two sisters embraced.

"Well, now, the tree looks just perfect," Mama said, beaming at her daughters. "Thank you so much, girls."

While the rest of the family admired the tree and the new glass ornaments, Fos and Tony were exploring the packages under its boughs. Finally, Fos could take it no more.

"Are we going to open our presents?" he burst out.

Papa laughed. "Of course! And since Hazel is too small yet to play Santa, that role falls to Tony Cole." The youngest Cole child always got to "play Santa" and distribute the packages under the tree to their owners.

Tony puffed out his chest with pride and walked over to the pile of presents, carefully considering his first move. After inspecting them, he skipped over the tantalizing large ones and pulled out the smallest package. He brought it over to Mama to read the label.

"Dock," she said. Tony importantly marched over to his oldest brother and handed him his present.

Dock took the small package and considered it for a second. He looked briefly out the window and gazed at the giant mounds of snow. "It's amazing that we can have Christmas after a storm like this," he said, looking at his parents. They smiled warmly in return.

Dock ripped at the fabric covering the small package and opened a delicate box. Inside was a silver pen. Ruble recognized it as one of the family's treasures, usually kept locked away in a drawer in her mother's room. Wrapped around the pen was a small note.

"What does it say?" Ruble asked.

"To our hard-working son," Dock read. "May this pen express your thoughts and embody your dreams. We are very proud of you."

Dock looked up at Mama, recognizing her penmanship on the note. When so few could read and write, his mother – who had finished the eighth grade – was highly educated. Dock had always considered the silver pen to be a symbol of his mother's quick mind. Though he had left school to work without complaint, Mama knew he was wistful of the time his siblings were granted to devote to their studies. His eyes shone brightly as he walked over to hug Mama and Papa. "Thank you," he whispered, holding the gifted pen.

"Next!" Fos called out impatiently, kicking his legs under his chair and eyeing the presents.

The next package Tony selected went to Maude. She pulled at the remnants of fabric and ribbon, opened the box, and gasped. "Mama! When did you have time…?" She pulled from the box a navy dress with deep red roses and held it up for all to see. It was the dress Maude had so admired only days before when Mama wore it to the Christmas party. It had been altered to fit Maude's slender frame and the sleeves refashioned to be more sleek and modern.

Mama beamed at Maude's surprised face. "I hope it fits all right," she said. "I thought maybe you could take it to college with you."

"It's wonderful, Mama," said Maude, moved to tears. "I don't know how you did it." As the two women embraced, Fos cleared his throat again, urging Tony on.

His younger brother obediently handed a package to Al, who quickly unfurled the fabric wrapping to reveal a hardback book. Ruble immediately recognized it, having seen it only two days before during the company Christmas party.

"The new book by John Fox Jr.!" he exclaimed, holding it up for all to see. Appreciative hoots greeted his announcement.

"We hope you'll read it to us tonight," Papa said from his chair where he was bouncing baby Hazel. Al had already cracked open the book and was eagerly flipping pages, as if trying to drink in the story. "I think he likes it, Mama," Papa said jubilantly.

The next package went to Hob. Observing Fos's impatience, Hob drew out the ceremony of unwrapping the present. First he shook the box, pretending to puzzle its contents. Then he slowly unwound the fabric wrapping, keeping the package mostly obscured.

"Oh, stop torturing Fos," Al called out.

Hob grinned, winked at Fos, and tore open the rest of the package. Inside was the whittling knife that Papa usually kept tucked in the pocket of his overalls.

"For carving," Papa said to Hob, walking over to him. "Now that you're old enough, I'll teach you, since you're interested."

Hob looked up at Papa and threw his arms around him. "I'm so glad," he said, inspecting the gleaming blade.

Fos cleared his throat again.

"I think Fos needs a present before he bursts," Papa said. "Tony, why don't you hand Fos that package and take the one next to it for yourself."

The two boys sat down with their presents, their faces lit up with excitement.

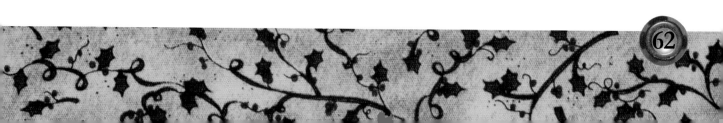

"On three," Fos instructed Tony. At the count of three, both boys tore open their gifts and simultaneously pulled out two hand-carved and hand-painted figures.

"A cowboy!" exclaimed Tony.

"A sheriff!" shouted Fos.

The two immediately started playing with their toys and Papa looked on in delight.

"Boys?" Mama called out. "Don't you want to say thank you? Your Papa carved those especially for you."

Fos and Tony ran to embrace Papa's long legs and he ruffled their hair lovingly.

"Now we have new men for our train heists!" Fos said happily. Then a thought occurred to him and he surveyed the remaining packages under the tree once

more. "I don't think I got my train," he said slowly.

Mama looked a little pained, and Papa reassuringly patted his head. Fos paused and tears welled up in his eyes. "I think I know why," he said quietly.

"Why is that?" Mama asked, pulling him onto her lap.

"I ate Tony's candy from his stocking yesterday," he confessed sadly. "I was bad." And with that, Fos burst into tears. "I'm sorry, Tony," he sobbed.

Tony, more distressed at seeing his big brother upset than at the loss of his candy, kindly patted Fos on his arm. "It's all right, Fos. I'm not mad."

Mama rocked Fos in her lap. "That wasn't a nice thing to do, Fos. But you're sorry and Tony forgives you. And I don't think Santa doesn't think you're a good boy. In fact, I know you're a very good boy."

Mama kissed Fos's forehead and held his little hand. "In fact, no one got any gifts from Santa this year." She smiled at the shocked expression on Fos's face, and Tony gasped. "And it's not because the Cole children aren't good children! Papa and I discussed it, and we think that Santa couldn't get to our house through this terrible storm. Imagine trying to find our house on this great big mountain through that snow and wind. I feel bad for Santa," Mama said seriously.

"Me, too," said Fos quietly.

"But I know you've been a good boy, because you still got a wonderful present, didn't you?" She pointed to the carved sheriff figure. Fos nodded his head, sniffling.

"Now," she said, kissing him once more, "don't you think you'll still have the best games, even without a new train?"

"Yes!" said Fos, his smile already returning. When Tony knocked his cowboy figure into Fos's sheriff in an invitation to spar, Fos scrambled off his mother's lap, playfully warning, "Watch it, outlaw."

The boys made a move for their toy chest and Ruble marveled at Fos's ever-buoyant spirit, but Mama stopped the boys in their tracks. "Christmas isn't finished yet, you two!" she said. "Ruble, Nelle, and Hazel need to open their gifts, and then we have the stockings to open."

"Yes," said Nelle. "And then we have a surprise for you and Papa!"

At that, Fos and Tony grinned and tucked their toys away. Tony resumed his work of passing out presents and everyone ooh'd and aah'd as Baby Hazel received a beautiful lacework bonnet. Ruble recognized her sister Maude's skilled craftsmanship in the small white knots and intricate eyelets. Mama immediately placed the hat on Hazel's small round head and Ruble walked over to pat her baby sister and plant a kiss on her chubby cheek. Then, finally, it was time for the last two Cole sisters to open their gifts.

"Ruble and Nelle, you should open these together," Mama said, pointing at two packages wrapped carefully in fabric.

Ruble studied the round package carefully and knew that her doll was not inside, but the realization didn't pain her, to her own surprise. She hadn't really expected to receive the expensive, store-bought doll for Christmas, and now she understood that she didn't need it. Looking around at the smiling faces of her family as they waited for her to open her gift, she realized she was already perfectly happy.

Ruble glanced at Nelle, who was balancing a matching package on her lap. "On three again?" Ruble asked merrily. Nelle beamed her assent.

Ruble gingerly pulled at the ribbon holding the fabric onto the package, savor-

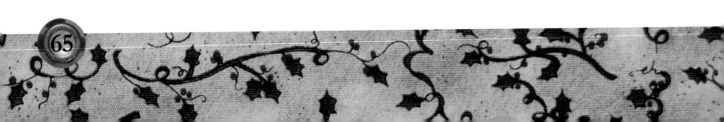

ing the moment. As one edge of the fabric slipped away, she saw a telltale deep purple surface gleaming through the gap she had made. Her breath caught and she turned to look at Nelle. Her sister's eyes had already pooled with tears and both girls moved their gazes to the empty top shelf of the family's bookcase.

The remaining purple carnival glass bowls were missing. Instead, the girls held them in their laps, delicately wrapped in fabric, a gift from Mama.

Ruble pulled away the rest of the fabric wrapping and held her purple dish up to the light. The sun shone through the window, and amplified by the snow, its beams glinted through the glass, painting a lavender stain on the wall behind Ruble.

Mama's voice spoke quietly from across the room. "A little bit of elegance for my elegant girls."

Nelle burst into happy sobs and clutched the bowl close to her chest.

Ruble beamed at her mother, who had shared one of her most prized treasures with her.

Mama crossed the room to embrace her two daughters. "Merry Christmas," she whispered as she hugged them. "Let these bowls be a reminder that I love you always and no matter what."

All around the room, members of the Cole family were admiring their gifts, all conceived and given with love. So satisfied were they that Mama had to prompt the family to open their stockings.

As soon as he retrieved his stocking from the mantle, Fos offered to give all his candy to Tony. "Take it, Tony," he said.

"No, Fos," Tony said seriously. "We'll share." The two brothers sat on the floor and divided pieces of Fos's broken candy cane with one of their hands, while battling cowboy and sheriff with their others.

At last, Nelle announced the nativity story would begin and Maude used a wet rag to wipe down her brothers' sticky mouths. Mama and Papa were made to wait in the bedroom while the children readied the "stage" for the Christmas story.

The rest of the afternoon was occupied with the children's play, which they performed for their delighted parents. Ruble's goat provided much comic relief by alternately trying to eat parts of the Christmas tree and Mary and Joseph's robes. "Another reason not to have goats in the house," Mama said in a mock stage whisper.

At the play's conclusion, all the Cole children bowed to their parents' sustained applause.

Nelle beamed at Mama and Papa. "I hope you enjoyed the play," she said. "I heard you say you liked the nativity story best of all, and we didn't want you to miss it."

Mama grinned. "This is the best nativity story I've ever seen performed," she said. "I had no idea I was bringing up a troupe of actors." Fos and Tony continued to take bows, to Papa's laughter, and Hob refused to remove his wise man costume the rest of the day.

The family then set to work preparing a Christmas feast and the house remained so warm and cozy that Ruble had to periodically press her face up to the frozen window to cool down. When her chores were finished, she organized the boys into a train heist on the living room floor, where she agreed to be tied to the tracks.

Hob was already hard at work trying to carve – he had even gone out into the cold to find a suitable stick to practice on. Al had his nose in his new book, and Dock was practicing his calligraphy with his new pen. Nelle and Maude stayed

in the cramped kitchen with Mama, laughing and talking about the nativity performance and helping to turn out the Christmas feast, and Papa took over the chores the children were neglecting and set up the supper table around the train heist.

Finally, after Christmas supper, when the stars were blinking in the dark sky, Al took his place in Mama's rocking chair to read to the family from his new book.

Ruble felt the day's excitement start to drain from her limbs. She leaned against Nelle, who threw a blanket around the two of them. She started to listen intently to Al's excited voice as he read from the book, but before long her eyelids began to droop. It wasn't until she felt Papa lift her into her bed that she realized she had fallen asleep.

"Merry Christmas, Tater," Papa whispered to her, kissing her on her forehead. As sleep took her, Ruble's thoughts drifted to her beautiful gifts – her deep purple glass bowl, her stocking full of goodies, and her father whispering goodnight to her – and she thought it might be the best Christmas ever.

Santa's Lost Sack

I t was a few days before the snow began to melt and the trains again rumbled down the tracks to Benham. School was closed because of the weather, and the children enjoyed their free time romping through the still-deep snow.

Hob was getting daily carving lessons from Papa and Mama shook her head at the stray wood shavings she found underfoot in every room of the house. Fos, Tony, and Ruble set up a fort in the living room where the sheriff, cowboy, and damsel in distress regularly performed. Al was nearly finished with his book, but he took time out to play an outlaw when needed. Maude and Nelle were busy sewing, preparing for Maude's departure for college in the spring. When he was not at work helping to clear the railroad tracks of snowdrifts, Dock practiced his penmanship with his new silver pen, which he kept carefully tucked away in his trunk when not in use.

When there was free time between chores, the children sometimes opened the wish book to gaze once more at its wonders. They never seemed to tire of their favorite game – how to spend twenty-four dollars – and even Fos and Tony had become adept at it. Al liked to spread out his imaginary money and buy as many items as possible. Ruble still occasionally turned to the dolls to gaze at her favorite, the one with yellow ringlets and the simple ruffled dress.

Eventually, the sun wore away the snow and the muddy paths to town became visible once more. The children made their way back to school and the Cole household returned to its familiar rhythms.

About two weeks after Christmas, Papa returned from the coal mine one night weighed down with packages. "The store finally got a mess of deliveries that were delayed by the storm," he explained, dropping sacks of corn meal, flour, and sugar onto the floor. "Practically nothing could get into town because of the snow. I couldn't believe how bare those store shelves were getting."

"Thank goodness," Mama said as she came in to retrieve the supplies. "Our own cupboards are practically bare."

"That's not my only good news, Mrs. Cole," Papa said, his eyes twinkling. "We also finally got the delivery we've been waiting for."

"What delivery?" interrupted Ruble, staring at her parents, who were now beaming happily.

"It's a surprise!" Papa laughed, startling Ruble by picking her up and twirling her. She giggled with astonishment at her father's unexplained good cheer.

Ruble thought Papa continued to act strangely joyous throughout the evening, occasionally grinning at his children without explanation, but he didn't mention the delivery or the surprise again. Still, Ruble watched Papa closely as he, Fos, Tony, and Hob played with their carved figures after supper.

"So, Fos Cole," Papa asked casually as he galloped an imaginary horse, "What do you think Santa did with the presents he couldn't deliver on Christmas morning?"

Fos looked up, puzzled. "I don't know, Papa," he said. "Do you?"

"Well, it's very mysterious," Papa intoned. "But I think I might know what happened. You see, I saw a strange sack in the cow barn this evening."

"What sack?" Hob asked.

"Well, it looked like it might be Santa's sack, but I didn't bother to open it,"

Papa said matter-of-factly. "I'm thinking maybe Santa did get lost in that blizzard on Christmas day. Otherwise, why would he have left that sack in the cow barn this afternoon?"

The children looked at him, eyes wide. "Maybe you all should go out and take a look," Papa said at last, his mouth twisting into a wide, mischievous grin.

"Can we go, Mama?" Hob burst out. Mama smiled indulgently and shooed the children out with her hands. They stumbled over one another to pile on hats, coats, and boots. Ruble grabbed Nelle's hand as they rushed out the door and the two of them skipped out across the yard, not feeling the cold.

When Dock dragged open the door to the cow barn, Ruble was surprised to see a large sack bulging with packages on the barn floor.

Tony stood back in awe as his siblings gathered around it. "Is it really from Santa?" he asked, bewildered and excited.

"I think it is," said Maude, examining it. "We'd better take it back into the house, don't you think?"

Dock and Al grabbed the sizable sack and the Cole children headed back into the warmth of the house. Mama and Papa were waiting expectantly around the Christmas tree, which was still lending its festive cheer to the living room.

"Papa, look!" Fos cried out, pointing to the sack. "More presents!"

Papa laughed merrily. He opened the sack that Dock and Al placed before him and jubilantly began to extract presents wrapped in colorful fancy paper. He handed a long box to Ruble and kissed her quickly on the cheek. "For you, Tater. Merry Christmas," he said.

Ruble's heart began to beat a little faster as she examined the present. She began to unwrap it, taking care not to rip the beautiful paper, which she set aside to use later. Then she slowly opened the long box. Inside, wrapped in tissue to preserve her appearance, was the doll Ruble had wished for in her letter to Santa.

Ruble gasped. She could hardly believe it, but there she was. Ruble gazed at her perfect yellow ringlets, painted blue eyes, and pretty dress. She pulled away the tissue paper and held the doll, amazed. "Thank you," she said aloud.

All around the room, Ruble's brothers and sisters were opening their gifts and finding inside the things they had requested from Santa from the wish book. Fos opened a box and found his train engine. Tony received his Lincoln Logs™, Maude discovered her fancy shoes, Al saw his new ice skates, Dock a BB gun, Nelle her baby doll, and Hob his slingshot. Even Hazel received new baby booties.

"A second Christmas!" Fos exclaimed, amazed.

Papa and Mama looked on with delight as their children examined their presents in wonder. Santa, it seemed, had been able to grant their wishes after all.

"So," Papa said at last. "What are everyone's favorite Christmas gifts?"

The children looked at one another, many still holding their newly unwrapped presents. Dock spoke first. "I like my new BB gun of course," he said. "But my favorite is my silver pen."

Maude nodded her head in agreement. "I never imagined I'd get these shoes," she said, holding them out for all to admire. "But my favorite Christmas present is my navy dress, definitely."

Nelle also looked at her mother and smiled. "My best Christmas gift ever is my carnival glass bowl," she said without hesitation. Nelle had set the purple dish in the windowsill of the children's bedroom and Ruble knew she gazed at it often.

Hob set down his new slingshot and held up the carving knife he kept in his pocket. "My favorite gift is my knife," he said. "And the lessons from you, Papa." His father grinned in return.

Tony had already set to work constructing a house with his Lincoln Logs, but he looked up as Papa asked him the same question. As an answer, he held up the carved cowboy he had carried around since Christmas day. "This is my favorite," he said, then turned back to his new Lincoln Logs. Papa laughed.

"Well, Fos?" he said, turning to the five-year-old. "What about you?"

Fos, for his part, looked troubled and confused. His mouth twisted into a frown and he gazed down at his lap, thinking hard. "I like them all!" he said at last. The family laughed at this answer.

"And what about you, Tater?" Papa looked to Ruble.

Ruble contemplated the doll in her hands, which she had thought she wouldn't receive. She thought of the purple glass bowl in the bedroom, which Mama had given to her with all her love. Then she looked into Papa's familiar face and saw him smile at her in anticipation. She knew her answer. "My best gift was Christmas morning, when Hilda bumped me out of bed again," she said.

The rest of the family laughed but Papa looked puzzled. "Whatever do you mean, Tater?"

Ruble's eyes shone as she gazed around the room at her family. "When Hilda pushed me out of bed, I knew you had let her in. And I knew you were safe. That was the best Christmas present I could have asked for."

Papa's eyes shone brightly at this unexpected answer. As he bent to hug Ruble, he whispered for a second time on this second Christmas, "Merry Christmas, Tater."

Ruble smiled.

THE END

EPILOGUE

The fall following that special Christmas, Maude entered Berea College under the tuition-free program provided to Appalachian students where she studied to become a teacher.

The Cole family lived in Benham, Kentucky, for eight years. At last, Mama told Papa to find less dangerous work; she didn't want to be a widow with nine children. Papa and Dock traveled ahead of the family to the Appalachian community of Norwood, Ohio, a city next to Cincinnati, where they found work as carpenters. Soon after, the rest of the Coles joined them and the family lived in a house that Dock and Papa built.

When the Great Depression struck, the family traded their house for a farm in nearby Loveland, Ohio. There, Papa became a successful farmer. The family lived for many years in Loveland, where they formed many more memories.

Since 1946, descendants of the Cole family have gathered every Father's Day for a reunion in Loveland on land that was once part of the family's farm. There are five living generations and 165 direct descendants of Mama and Papa Cole.

A Note on the Fabric Borders

Mama Cole's quilt (above) provided inspiration for the design of *Cole Family Christmas*. The six vintage Christmas-themed fabrics featured on the borders of this book are similar to fabrics that Mama Cole would have used to construct the family's quilts.

Our Family

1919 — Benham, Kentucky

Standing: John Westerfield Cole (Dock), Maude Elizabeth Cole, Nelle Lee Cole

Front row: Charles Hobert Cole (Hob), Mama, George Foster Cole (Fos), Papa, Joseph Henry Cole (Tony), Ruble Aleen Cole, James Albert Cole (Al)

DEDICATION

We would like to dedicate this work to the family of Joseph Henry (1881-1970) and Martha Jane nee Baker (1884-1961) Cole.

No opportunity has seemed too far for your reach and no lesson too distant to learn. We are so very fortunate that your genes are among ours.